pincushion
sewing
basket
suitcase
purse
charm
bracelet
locket
puzzles
golf clubs
Teddy bear
rake
flower
seeds
flowerpots
watering
can
wheel-
barrow
Pony
cowboy hat
BIKE
hula
hoop
clown
suit
peanuts
elephant
monkey
safari
hat
butterfly
net

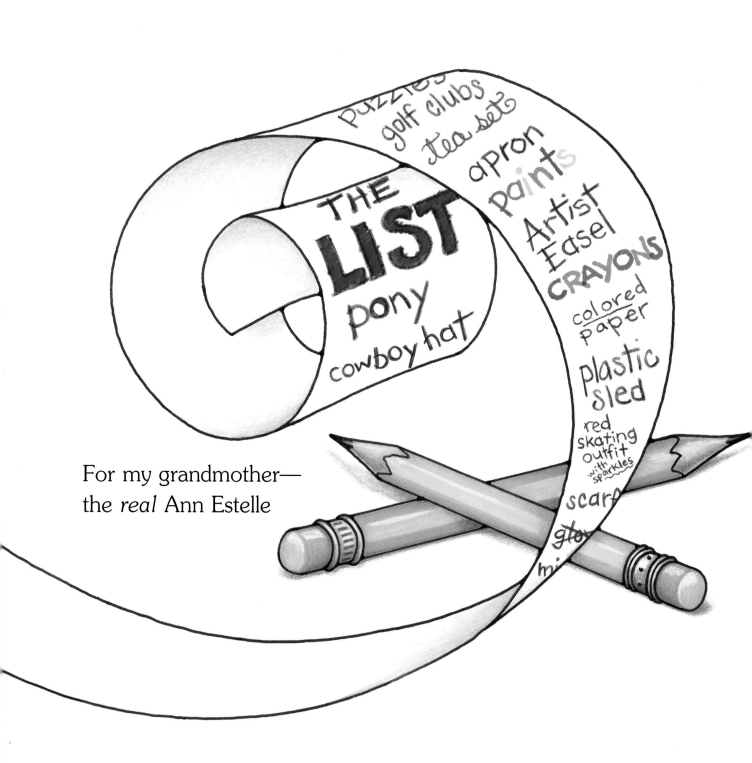

For my grandmother—
the *real* Ann Estelle

ANN ESTELLE STORIES

Queen of Christmas

BY MARY ENGELBREIT

HarperCollinsPublishers

hristmas was only **7** days away. As the self-appointed Queen of Christmas, Ann Estelle had a lot to do to make sure everything went exactly the way she wanted. So many wonderful things happened around Christmastime, she didn't want to miss anything! But the most important thing, at least in Ann Estelle's mind, was . . .

The List.

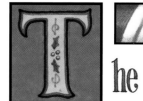 **he List** was a very, *very* long piece of paper on which Ann Estelle had written every single solitary item she had ever wanted or could even imagine wanting at some later date. She had started The List right after Christmas last year.

I t was a little long, but she couldn't see wasting a golden gift-getting opportunity like Christmas.

Christmas was only **6** days away. Ann Estelle and her mother got ready to make gazillions of cookies as they did every year for friends and family. It was so much fun that Ann Estelle almost forgot The List. But then she had a thought. Shouldn't the Queen of Christmas have her very own apron just her size?

Ann Estelle added an *apron* fit for a queen to The List. She was happy to see there was a little more room left in case she thought of anything else.

Christmas was only **5** days away. It snowed and snowed. Ann Estelle and her father got out the old wooden sled that had been his when he was little. It was the best sled in the world and went down the hill just as fast as could be.

But still, Ann Estelle thought it would be nice to have a brand-new plastic sled. She put it on The List as soon as they got home.

Christmas was only **4** days away. Ann Estelle's grandmother was coming to stay for the whole rest of Christmas vacation! Ann Estelle loved her grandmother. She couldn't wait to go ice-skating with her, as they did every year when she visited.

When they got to the ice rink, her grandmother showed her how to do figure eights.

Ann Estelle thought she would do figure eights much better in a sparkly red skating outfit. She decided to squeeze a red skating outfit—with sparkles—onto The List.

Christmas was only **3** days away. The Queen of Christmas built a magnificent snowman, with a carrot nose, black button eyes, and a warm woolen hat. He was even better than the snowman she built last year.

**U**nfortunately, Ann Estelle lost a mitten in the snow. Oh well, she said to herself. She'd just put **mittens** on The List.

C hristmas was only **2** days away. Ann Estelle's family, of course, went caroling with all their neighbors, just as they did every year. It was so much fun! The Queen wore her Christmas crown and sang the loudest of anyone.

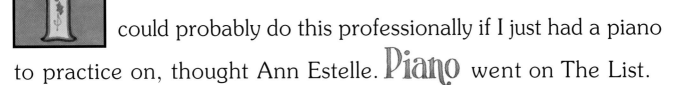

I could probably do this professionally if I just had a piano to practice on, thought Ann Estelle. *Piano* went on The List.

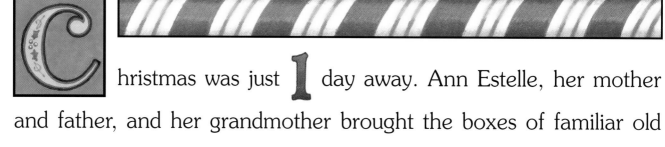

Christmas was just **1** day away. Ann Estelle, her mother and father, and her grandmother brought the boxes of familiar old ornaments up from the basement.

It took all day to decorate the tree because friends kept dropping by to say "Merry Christmas!" Ann Estelle thought there had probably never been a Christmas Eve that was so much fun.

nn Estelle hadn't thought about The List all day. Right before bed her father reminded her to leave it next to Santa's milk and plate of cookies. Ann Estelle read it over carefully. She hoped she hadn't forgotten anything because that would make Christmas not quite as wonderful as it should be.

As she tapped her pencil against her lip, her father politely cleared his throat. "Well," said Ann Estelle, "I guess I've done all I can do here to make Christmas perfect. Good night, everybody!" And with that, The List was finally finished.

On Christmas morning, Ann Estelle ran downstairs to see what Santa had brought. Even though she didn't get everything on her list, she was surprised to find that the gifts she did get were absolutely perfect!

And just as Ann Estelle finished opening her presents, all of her aunts and uncles and cousins arrived. The Christmas celebration began in earnest!

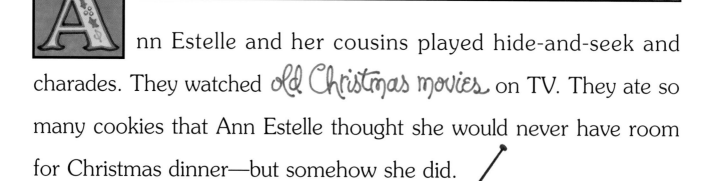

nn Estelle and her cousins played hide-and-seek and charades. They watched *old Christmas movies* on TV. They ate so many cookies that Ann Estelle thought she would never have room for Christmas dinner—but somehow she did.

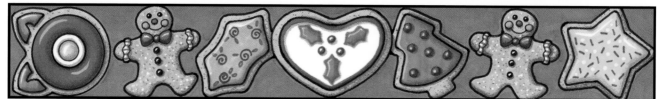

Late that night, after singing carols and telling stories, everyone went home. Ann Estelle's parents finally tucked her into bed. "It was Christmas exactly the way I wanted it," said Ann Estelle to her mother and father as she curled up under the covers. "Ice-skating with Grandma, baking the cookies, Christmas caroling, decorating the tree . . ."

**W**hat about the presents you got that were on your list?" whispered her father as he turned out the light.

"Oh, Dad," said Ann Estelle, "it's not just the presents that matter. Don't you know that?"

He kissed her, but the Queen of Christmas had fallen asleep without thinking of even one thing to put on next year's list.

Queen of Christmas
Copyright © 2003 by M. E. Enterprises, Inc.
Manufactured in China. All rights reserved.

www.harperchildrens.com

Library of Congress Cataloging-in-Publication Data

Engelbreit, Mary.
Queen of Christmas / by Mary Engelbreit.—1st ed.
p.   cm. — (Ann Estelle stories)
Summary: Although Ann Estelle focuses on her wish
list as Christmas approaches, her best memories have
little to do with the presents she receives.
ISBN 0-06-008175-9 — ISBN 0-06-008176-7 (lib. bdg.)
[1. Christmas—Fiction. 2. Gifts—Fiction.] I. Title.

PZ7.E69975 Qs 2003
[E]—dc21   2002038802

Typography by Stephanie Bart-Horvath
1 2 3 4 5 6 7 8 9 10
❖
First Edition